THE MYSTERY OF THE POLLUTED STREAM

WRITTEN BY MARY BLOUNT CHRISTIAN
ILLUSTRATED BY JOE BODDY

Milliken Publishing Company, St. Louis, Missouri

Cover Design by Henning Design, St. Louis, Missouri

Library of Congress Catalog Card Number: 90-064480

ISBN 0-88335-2990 (lib. bdg.) 0-88335-2907 (pbk.)

Walter's dog Watson dashed ahead of him through the tall grass, growling and chasing grasshoppers.

Ann, David, and Pedro followed Walter on the footpath, which was muddy from three days' heavy rain. The path led to a small stream which emptied into Doyle Lake, fifteen miles away.

"Silly dog," Ann said. "You'll crush all the pretty wildflowers, thrashing around like that."

1

"That was the hardest rain I can remember," David said. "I hope we can find some tadpoles in the stream."

"Yes," Pedro told the twins. "Several days ago we cleaned the old fish tank at school and filled it with water. Now that the water is ready we can put rocks, plants, and the tadpoles in it. Then the whole class can watch the tadpoles develop into frogs."

2

"Don't forget to put a top over the fish tank," Ann said, laughing. "We forgot last year, and we had tiny frogs hopping all over the classroom."

Suddenly the children stopped and wrinkled their noses. "Oooh," Pedro said. "What's that awful smell?"

Watson sneezed, then ran to stand behind Walter.

Cautiously, the children crept toward the smell. "Look!" Ann said, pinching her nose. "There are dead fish in the water and on the banks. Ugh!"

David scooped his jar into the water. The water looked dark and ugly. It smelled bad, too.

"I think the Sherlock Street Detectives should investigate," Ann said.

The stream was moving slowly, and the children couldn't tell which direction it was flowing. David picked a leaf from a nearby tree. He tossed it into the water. The children watched it float east. "The pollution must be coming from that direction. We can backtrack and find where the fish kill starts."

"Let's go back to the house, David," Walter said. "You should wash your hands. Then we had better call the City Environmental Department to investigate."

The others agreed. While David washed his hands, Walter reported the dead fish. Then they rejoined Ann and Pedro.

6

The four detectives walked upstream. They saw fish floating on the water as far as they could see.

They walked past neighborhoods, a shopping center, a farm, and an industrial park. Finally, they found clear water.

"The pollution must start below here," David said. "But what caused it?"

Ann crossed her arms. "I bet it's that service station. Its gas tanks may be leaking. I'm always seeing news about fuel spills."

"Gasoline would leave a shiny film on top of the water, Ann," Walter said.

"Yeah, right," she said. "We should check, though."

"I could tell the stream was smelling bad," the service station manager said when they told him about the fish kill.

"Maybe your gas tanks are leaking," Ann said.

"No," the manager said. "We have new tanks, and we have been inspected for leaks in the past few months. Something else must be causing the fish kill."

9

"Maybe it's coming from the industrial park," Pedro said. "There's a dry cleaning plant there. And there's a pulp paper company. Both of those use chemicals that could kill fish."

"We use many chemicals," the man at the dry cleaners said. "But trucks take the liquids to places for safe disposal. We are good neighbors and we are very careful."

Next the children went to the pulp paper company.

"We need water to make pulp from wood fibers," the manager said. "But we use the same water over and over."

He showed the children the holding tanks. "We have filters to clean the water. See that yellow sludge?" he said, pointing. "If it was our pollution, the stream would be yellow. It wasn't yellow, was it?"

"No," David said. "The water looked muddy. But it didn't look yellow."

"We try to take care of the environment," the manager said. "You'll have to look somewhere else for the source."

13

The children walked toward home. " [ ] a truck from the city!" Ann said. "It ha[ ] green tree on the side. It must be fr[ ] the City Environmental Department.[ ]

14

They hurried to where the truck was parked. A woman wearing protective gloves was dipping glass vials into the water. Carefully she covered the vials, then she put them inside plastic bags. She labeled each bag.

A man who was also wearing protective gloves was collecting dead fish and putting them into plastic bags.

15

The woman looked up. "Are you the kids who reported the fish kill?" she asked.

"Yes," Walter said. "We are the Sherlock Street Detectives. We tried to find the reason for the fish kill. We went to the service station, the dry cleaning company, and the pulp paper company."

"Everything seemed all right at those places," Ann said.

The woman nodded and smiled at them. "We will know for sure when we test our samples."

Ann pointed. "Look," she said. "I see a tank truck over there on that farm."

"You have sharp eyes," the woman said. "Let's talk to the farmer. We may learn something."

17

The Sherlock Street Detectives walked with the woman, carefully stepping over the rows of plants. Their sneakers sank deeply into the mud between the rows.

As they got closer to the tank truck, Pedro said, "Look at the truck. There's a skull and crossbones on the side. That's the sign for danger."

"Hello," the woman called out to the two men standing in the field. She waved at them.

One of the men waved back and walked toward them, his hand extended in greeting. The two shook hands. "I'm Sue Clark with the City Environmental Department," she said. "And these young folks are the Sherlock Street Detectives."

"Sam Hayward," the man said, nodding to the children. "This is my farm. What can I do for you?"

"There's been a big fish kill on the stream behind your farm," Ms. Clark said. "It goes for miles."

19

"I wondered what that smell was," Mr. Hayward said. "But why are you here?"

"We are looking for the source of the kill," Ms. Clark told him.

Mr. Hayward frowned. "I'm a farmer," he said. "I grow vegetables. You should look for oil spills or stuff like that."

Ms. Clark nodded. "Yes sir. We'll look into everything. I see you have a truck here to apply insecticide to your plants."

"Yes," Mr. Hayward said. "The bugs will eat my crops if I don't spray them."

"I thought perhaps you sprayed your crops before the rain," Ms. Clark said.

"Oh!" Ann said. "You think the rain washed the insecticide into the stream and killed the fish!"

Ms. Clark turned to look at her.

"Ooops," Ann said. "Sorry. I didn't mean to interrupt."

"This is my first spray of the season," Mr. Hayward said. "I knew from the weather forecast that we were due for some rain. I waited until it was over. I can't afford to spray twice."

"I'm glad to hear that you didn't spray already," Ms. Clark said. "Still it is possible that the stream is contaminated from years and years of insecticide. We'll know more when we test the water."

j42276

"I hope not," Mr. Hayward said. "I don't want to kill fish and ruin a stream."

"Plant onions with your crops!" Pedro said. "Bugs hate onions and garlic. That keeps them away from the other plants, too!"

Mr. Hayward looked at Pedro. "Are you sure?"

"Sure," Pedro said. "My parents run a nursery. That's what they do to keep the plants free of bugs. It doesn't hurt the environment, and we have onions to eat, too."

Ms. Clark patted Pedro on the shoulder. "He's right. There are other things you can do, too. Someone from our department will visit you soon. We'll tell you ways to keep your crops healthy and still be a good neighbor."

The children walked with Ms. Clark back to her truck. "Thanks for your help, kids," she said. She promised to let them know when she found the cause of the fish kill.

25

The Sherlock Street Detectives were having lemonade several weeks later when Ms. Clark came by. Ann poured her a glass. "Was it insecticide that killed the fish?" Ann asked.

"Or cleaning solution?" Walter guessed.

"Or. . ." Pedro said.

Ms. Clark held up her hand. "You could guess all day. There are so many ways we can hurt our streams. But this time it was Mother Nature herself," she said.

"What?" all four children asked at once. "How?"

"Have you ever forgotten to clean a fish tank?" Ms. Clark asked. "Dirt builds up in the bottom and if the water gets stirred up, the fish get sick and die. The same thing happened in the stream."

"There were years and years of sediment on the bottom of the stream. The heavy rains stirred up the sediment. It came to the top and made the fish sick."

"But the stream is a body of moving, living water!" Pedro said.

"Right!" Ms. Clark said. "But the rain also caused old tree limbs and brush to float away. They stopped under bridges and clogged the stream's progress."

"I guess the Sherlock Street Detectives learned something this time after all," David said. "We learned we must gather all the facts first."

"And not leap to conclusions," Walter added.

"And that clean water is something special," Ann said, lifting her glass of lemonade.

"Right!" the others agreed, lifting their glasses, too.

Glossary

contaminate — to make impure, to pollute

environment — the living things that make up a community

insecticide — a chemical that kills insects

sediment — solid matter that settles to the bottom of a liquid

Vocabulary

Ann	danger	guess	plastic	stream(s)
apply	David	Hayward	pointing	tadpoles
backtrack	department	healthy	pollution	tank(s)
banks	detectives	heavy	possible	thrashing
bridges	develop	hopping	progress	twins
brush	dipping	hurried	promised	upstream
carefully	direction	industrial	protective	vegetables
cautiously	disposal	insecticide	pulp	vials
chemicals	Doyle	inside	rejoined	Walter
children	emptied	inspected	reported	Watson
Clark	environment	investigate	samples	weathercast
classroom	extended	lemonade	sank	wildflowers
cleaners	farmer	limbs	scooped	wrinkled
cleaning	fibers	liquids	sediment	
clogged	filled	manager	service	
collecting	filters	muddy	several	
company	flowing	mystery	Sherlock	
conclusions	footpath	nature	shopping	
contaminated	frowned	neighbor	shoulder	
covered	fuel	nodded	skull	
crept	garlic	nursery	sludge	
crop(s)	gather	oil	sneakers	
crossbones	grasshoppers	onions	solution	
crossed	greeting	Pedro	sprayed	
crush	growling	pinching	station	